Sarratt and the Draper of Watford

by John le Carré

and other unlikely stories about Sarratt
from international authors

CONTENTS

Enclosure: The People of Sarratt Midsummer's Day, 21 June 1999

FOREWORD

May I recommend this book to you.

I am sure you will find it entertaining with five quite different stories.

I believe it is also a "first" - it being an original example of village enterprise in order to raise funds for two local charities.

Finally, I must declare an interest – I live in Sarratt!

Morton Neal

CHESS VALLEY BY JAN CLUTTERBUCK

There has never been a spy school in the village of Sarratt, Hertfordshire, nor, as far as we know, did the KGB ever single out a grave in the village church for a dead letter drop. But in this unique collection, a captivating English village is transformed by the writer's imagination into "a kind of secret haven" as intriguing as the ancient history of Sarratt itself. The purpose of the book, which was inspired by John le Carré's fictional depiction of Sarratt as the location of a training school for spies, is to raise funds to preserve the village heritage for future generations.

"Sarratt and the Draper of Watford" brings together for the first time the writings of two men who are no longer separated by an Iron Curtain following the disintegration of Communist rule in the former Soviet Union – John le Carré, one of Britain's most eminent writers of spy fiction, and the former KGB Colonel Mikhail Lyubimov.

Sarratt appears in both stories both as a real village and as a symbolic place reflecting the character's own circumstances in life. As le Carré writes in his story "Sarratt and the Draper of Watford", "Sarratt impressed itself upon me as some kind of secret haven, a forgotten piece of real England just round the corner from subtopia." The central character in Col. Lyubimov's story, the fictional "Colonel Karla", sees the village as a tranquil rural backwater; a place to while away one's retirement, "recalling from time to time a glorious past of espionage". Col. Lyubimov's story, "The Adventures of Colonel Karla in Sarratt", is mainly a light-hearted depiction of an incident in the life of an intelligence agent in London, reflecting Lyubimov's own dry sense of humour. But there are darker undertones too, with the reflections on Sarratt evoking Colonel Karla's longings for a world of private intimacy, away from the "eternal snows" of Moscow. Alexander Norman's profile of Colonel Lyubimov on p. 54 of this collection gives a fascinating insight into the hidden world of an ex-KGB operative.

The visitor to Sarratt today can experience the same sense of awe as John le Carré did in the Church of the Holy Cross, which the writer perceived as one of the "keepers of an English mystery". The village of Sarratt grew as a cluster of houses around this 12th century church, and a rare mural dating back to this period and depicting a scene from the life of Christ is still visible on one of the walls. Historians believe that the purpose of the mural was to transmit the teachings of the Bible to illiterate villagers through images of the transcendent. The Church of the Holy Cross also contains ancient graffiti of a less sublime nature – a rough design for a noughts and crosses-type game dating back to the medieval period is scrawled upon another wall.

The survival of the church intact today is a testimony to the energy and dedication of the Victorian architect Sir Gilbert Scott and one of the vicars of the church Edward Ryley, who served as Rector from 1859-1912. Under the guidance of Sir Gilbert, Rev. Ryley saved the church from collapse and dereliction; his personal account of the history of the church appears on p. 59 of this book. Rev. Ryley, whose obituary in the Watford Observer in 1912 said that he was "in every sense the father of the village", was devoted to the church, and his writings reflect his love of the village and surrounding countryside. "Walking to the church from Chorleywood," wrote a member of the local history society in 1902, "You cross lush meadows, where cattle sometimes stand bathed in grass to the dewlap, to the River Chess – the happy, literary, trout-haunted, sparkling Chess, the banks of which are still yellow here and there with mimulus". Visitors to Sarratt today can still enjoy walks through unspoilt countryside; the parish of Sarratt has a network of 68 paths covering 26 miles through the valley of the River Chess.

The aim of this book is to provide funds for two charities, The Friends of Holy Cross Church and The Sarratt Village Hall Trust, with the proceeds of the sales shared equally. The Friends of Holy Cross Church (Registered Charity No. 1018991) continues the heritage of restoration that the Rev. Ryley embarked upon a century ago. At present the church is in need of extensive repairs to the roof. Likewise, there is constant expenditure required to maintain the church in a sound condition necessary for any building that is more than 800 years old. The Sarratt Village Hall Trust (Registered Charity No. 302464) has embarked upon a project to redevelop and enlarge the present village hall at a cost of £430,000. While certain grants have been received a great deal of funding is still required. All of the writers featured in the book generously donated their stories in aid of the appeal.

Contributors to this collection are from all over the world. John le Carré is based in Cornwall, while Colonel Lyubimov writes fiction in his apartment in Moscow or his dacha in the Russian countryside. The US author Kurt Willinger currently lives in Connecticut, and William Petre, the son of an old Bailey judge, is a young writer from London. Alexander Norman also lives in London. The author of the entertaining short story "A Local Affair" prefers to remain anonymous!

In all the stories the place names are real and in some cases so are the names of characters. Events are fictitious, except in the John le Carré story – where everything, almost, is true!

The book is illustrated by work from three of the most eminent of the many local artists – Agnes Bantock, Gillian Burrows and Jan Clutterbuck.

If you have already bought this book we thank you on behalf of The Friends of Holy Cross Church and The Sarratt Village Hall Trust. If you are considering its purchase, we commend it to you – the le Carré story alone is a classic of its time.

Kate Saunders

Kate Saunders is a writer and researcher specialising in Tibet and China. Her book, Eighteen Layers of Hell: Stories from the Chinese Gulag *was published by Cassell in 1996. Kate's articles have been published in newspapers and magazines worldwide including* The Independent, The Guardian *and* The Washington Post.

CHILTERN LANDSCAPE BY GILLIAN BURROWS

9

John le Carré

John le Carré was born on 1931. After attending the universities of Bern and Oxford, he taught at Eton and spent five years in the British Foreign Service.

His third novel, The Spy Who Came In From The Cold, *secured him a wide reputation which was consolidated by the acclaim for his trilogy,* Tinker Tailor Soldier Spy, The Honourable Schoolboy *and* Smiley's People. *His most autobiographical novel,* A Perfect Spy, *was followed by* The Russia House, The Secret Pilgrim, The Night Manager, Our Game, The Tailor of Panama *and* Single & Single, *his seventeenth novel.*

John le Carré lives in Cornwall.

Writers seldom know why they do things until they get smart afterwards, and I am no exception. So a big caution notice should be attached to what follows. Why on earth, you ask, did I choose the beautiful village of Sarratt for the setting of my unlovely British spy school?

The reasons, as they appear to me with the convenience of hindsight a quarter of a century later, are twofold:

I should never have said 'yes' to the gimlet-eyed lady on the ski slopes of the Bernese Oberland in – I fear – 1949.

I should never have coveted a thirty-pound charcoal grey suit with two vents and narrow trousers, displayed in the window of Messrs. Clements of Watford, Drapers, property of my friend Dick Edmonds.

* * *

The gimlet-eyed lady was fearless, formidable, eccentric, upper-class and athletic. She had a ten-acre voice, a rich husband in the City, and a will of iron. Even in the ski costume of fifty years ago, she was dauntingly thin.

I was a flaxen, pink-faced, easily embarrassed eighteen-year-old, inclined to poetry and puppy fat. I had recently defected from an English public school I loathed, and embarked on a course of study at Bern university. And I had never in my life met anyone as forceful as the gimlet-eyed lady.

"Don't be *utterly* ridiculous", she told me, in cadences similar to those later employed by Britain's first woman Prime Minister. "It will do you the *world* of good, and you'll be serving your *country.*"

In 1949 everyone of my age wanted to serve his country because we felt so uncomfortable about not having fought in the war. So maybe she got me on the war-guilt ticket. But far more likely is, I hadn't the bottle to say no to her.

However it was, moments later I had agreed to become a trainee ski racer under the aegis of something called the Downhill Only Club, which has its soul in the mountain village of Wengen. No decision in my later life – whether in the army, at university, in the secret world or in the pursuit of love – was ever so frivolously or impulsively taken.

None exposed me to such naked humiliation, or entirely justified terror.

Yet without it I would never have met Dick Edmonds and would never have signed on for three weeks' hard labour as a towel & carpet salesman for the Grand Summer Sale at Dick's family firm, Clements of Watford, known also – do they still use the same slogan? – as The Harrods of Hertfordshire.

Dick was already Crown Prince of Clements and Supreme Ruler Designate. The King himself had retired to his estates in Gloucestershire where he stocked the river with trout and swished his tail from time to time but was otherwise quiescent. And if I hadn't met Dick and heard of Clements, I would not have gone to Watford or coveted the twin-vented, narrow-trousered charcoal suit in the window without which I knew, as soon as I set eyes on it, my life would never be complete.

For Dick too had somehow been talked into becoming a fellow trainee. Even debonair Dick, vastly more worldly than myself and already in possession of an Army commission and brass-buttoned blazer to match, not to mention an Oxford degree, a Triumph Roadster and a well-developed sense of his own value to society, had not mustered the gall to say "no" to the gimlet-eyed lady. Perhaps the subsidised rates had attracted him. Or the girls. Dick in those days was definitely not impervious to either. Perhaps he even had a genuine desire to excel as a ski-racer, though I severely doubt it. For Dick, if you know your P.G. Wodehouse, was my Uckridge, my surfer over life's inconvenient hummocks – if not quite in the sense that the gimlet-eyed one might have wished. Or perhaps, since Dick was never so easily read, there did indeed lurk in him some patriotic impulse that obliged him to heed the Great Call. Ours not to reason why.

* * *

I recall vividly our first meeting as, pale and apprehensive, we sank our fitness beers and dragged at our fitness cigarettes in the Eiger bar in Wengen. The scene resembles in my memory the meeting of two fugitives to the French Foreign Legion as they crouch shoulder to shoulder in the waiting room of the recruitment office in Marseilles, assuring each other that things weren't going to be as bad as they were cracked up to be.

They were worse.

To appreciate the lunacy of our situation you must see a rabble of unfit, unskilled, Sunday morning soccer players drafted, by a quirk of divine malice, to play a season's worth of American football in the top league. With one exception we were, as I recall, without a spark of skiing talent.

Speaking for myself, I am afflicted with some kind of English pelvic deformity most commonly acquired at public school or inculcated by nannies which now, as then, prevents me from turning to my right without a convulsive jerk of the left elbow.

Dick, when I last saw him ski, resembled an avenging Sydney Bridge in a Spielberg science fiction movie. He was no different fifty years ago, except that there was a predatory glint in his eye, and a certain dihedral to the nose, which implied that the race was already won, and he was just dropping in to collect the prize.

Few of us had more than four or five seasons to our credit. And for season, read two sybaritic weeks in any one year. Never mind. Our love of country, our sportsmanship, our innate superiority as Brits of a certain class – didn't we teach these bloody foreigners how to ski in the first place? – would see us through.

Or would it? Remember, please, that in the early post-war years of skiing, safety-bindings were virtually unknown. The "Club Binding", as it was grandly titled, was a thirty centime ski-strap looped round the cable of the standard Kandahar binding and screwed with your penknife to the ski. If you fell forward and the wind was in the right direction, it might work. But we fell in all the directions of the compass, on whatever part of us hit the slopes first, and the best we could pray for was that the ski broke before we did. It was not long, therefore, before our motivation was on a par with our ability: why go faster when faster means breaking more limbs?

And then there was our splendid English competitive spirit. "But to compete!" ran the great slogan – whose I forget – but it was trumpeted around with Messianic fervour by the gimlet-eyed lady and her kind, as I'm sure it was in the Light Brigade Mess when one or two backsliders suggested it might not be such a great idea to charge the guns at Sebastapol.

How on earth do you preserve your competitive spirit when you know that any ten-year-old native child in the village can out-ski you in his sleep? – let alone the super-trained, mountain-bred international gods dreaming of Olympic gold, whose names, known to numberless fans, featured in alphabetical order alongside your own on the start list? For years I kept those start lists as testimony to my finest hours. For some reason, I never kept the results.

John le Carré (left) and Dick Edmonds skiing in the fifties.

* * *

How much of the bleak reality of our predicament Dick and
I communicated to one another is now mercifully unknown to me.
We were good soldiers but we could still count the numbers of our English
dead. A couple of our group wisely quit the field ahead of being cut down,
mumbling things about sick relatives or matters of business to attend to.
One brave fellow simply packed and tiptoed out of the hotel at dead of
night. I am sure I wished secretly that I had the courage to follow his
example, but I hadn't. And as the team was steadily whittled down, Dick
and I and a couple of other pseudo good-sports became by attrition its
surviving members, now cursing our misfortune as yet another awful
race-day loomed, now feebly aping our Battle of Britain rôle-models as
we staggered onto the scaffold and submitted to the executioner's chant
of "Eins, zwei, drei, *los*" before hurling ourselves down the precipice to
the greater glory of nobody, least of all ourselves.

But we survived – or Dick and I did. Both of us were natural survivors,
both of us knew that good men were scarce. Dick, so far as I remember,
won nothing, which was a given from the start, but also broke nothing
except a heart or two. The Sydney Bridge technique that has since taken
him safely over countless glaciers, ice fields and virgin slopes in the High
Alps took him down the race courses also, a lesson to all of us that, in
skiing as in life, what looks best may not work best, and vice versa. I too
won nothing, except a good friend and, since I had no money and no
clothes, an invitation to come and sell towels in Clements' Summer Sale
in exchange for a charcoal grey suit with two vents and narrow trousers.

* * *

If you have ever crouched unarmed in a shallow trench with a forest
full of wolves behind you and ahead of you glistening squadrons of enemy
cavalry advancing at full gallop with sabres drawn, then you will have
some inkling of how it feels to be standing on the receiving side of the
towels and white linen counter as the shop doors open on the first day
of a Summer Sale. It was only as I saw the barbarian hoards advancing

on me that I recognised the inescapable link between downhill ski-racing and what Dick in draper mode deprecatingly used to call flogging knickers in Watford High Street. Whether you are behind the counter or on the piste: it is the same daredevil sensation of watching yourself hurtle into catastrophe without the least control over your fate.

And catastrophe on that First Day Of Sale came to me in the unlikely form of a very small German lady in a tartan overcoat and battered brown bowler hat. She was sixty if a day, but she slipped out of the scrum like a champion to stand sovereign and motionless before me, or rather below me, a tiny, wrinkled genie with a face like a polished walnut and a gaze every bit as imperious as that of the gimlet-eyed one on the ski slopes in the Bernese Oberland, while all around her an inferno of larger, less agile bodies writhed and moaned and struck in the endless human battle for fifty percent off retail price to clear.

And when she spoke, her voice would have done credit to a sergeant major of the Kaiser's Imperial Prussian Guard on a good day, for the entire store heard her, and for a second froze as if to her command.

"College boy," she cried. The college boy was me. "Please, darling. I vant a towel for a guest".

The entire store stayed frozen, waiting breathless for my reply. Perhaps they knew her. Perhaps she was a great star – of the opera, the stage, the silver screen. I'll never know and I certainly didn't know then. All I knew, or thought I knew, was that everyone – babes in prams, bridal couples, seasoned sale-goers and shoplifters – all of them were waiting on me to come up with some kind of reciprocity of scale, some awareness of a great occasion.

"Madam," I replied finally, in tones that I hoped were as momentous as her own: "What size is your guest?"

Justice at Clements in those days was swift, and administered with a stern hand. The Chief Linen Buyer was a stately Irishman named Mr. Chase, and Mr. Chase was a salesman to his bushy eyebrows and bald pate. As a child Mr. Chase had lisped in discounts; at school, I have no doubt he had eagerly frequented the great sales psychologists. Only that morning, while the queues were forming round the block, Mr. Chase had initiated me into the arts of converting factory-bound bundles of new

16

linen into ragged heaps of apparently rejected treasures as a means of whetting the appetites of our customers.

The German lady had found Mr. Chase as swiftly as she had found me. She stood no higher than his waist, yet the two of them bore down on me with the majesty of their combined authority.

"You're fired," Mr. Chase informed me in a voice of thunder, while at the same time tipping me the fattest wink this side of the Irish Sea.

"You'd better try carpets," said Dick, as if carpets were the one place where I could be relied upon not to set the shop on fire.

He was mistaken. The very next day I sold the same twelve-foot strip of ex-Queen Elizabeth carpet to twenty different customers on the erroneous assumption that it was a sample and there was plenty more of it knocking around the warehouse.

There was none.

* * *

The Queen Elizabeth in her hey-day changed her carpets every couple of years, and Clements were proud of offering the best of what was discarded. Mr. Seaholm, the Chief Carpet Buyer, was particularly proud and had caused advertisements to this effect to be placed in the local newspaper. The Queen Elizabeth carpets were a Clements come-on, a perfectly legitimate one, intended to characterise the Sale. Who could have imagined that the few bits on offer in the basement were all that remained to use once the vomit stains and cigar burns had been weeded out? Nobody had told me, in as many words, that the piece I had sold so many times was a sample, but my imagination had left me in no doubt. After all, it was a huge ship with endless corridors. It was not the last time that my imagination turned out to be a wrecker's lamp.

Have you ever seen a Chief Carpet Buyer weep? For weeks after the sale, as Dick never tired of telling me, Clements was obliged to devote its considerable legal and diplomatic resources to repairing the mayhem I had left behind. Enraged housewives were mollified with other carpets – at sacrificial prices. The litigious were appeased with gifts and crawling letters of apology. An inexperienced anonymous salesman no longer in the firm's employment was identified as the culprit, and Dick gave me a year to pay off my charcoal grey suit.

And as a last charitable gesture, Dick in his magnanimity commissioned a mural from me, to adorn a large area of wall in the main concourse. Perhaps he had concluded that our relationship was best preserved if he became a patron of my art. I drew it, I painted it, and for a year or so – but less perhaps, for Dick was always keen to spare my feelings on the matter – it remained there. A pageant, I liked to think, of happy Watford shoppers trooping gaily through Clements' portals and trooping out of them again even happier than when they entered. Until a day came when Dick's father paid a visit to the store and summarily ordered my mural removed on the grounds that it insulted the customers. I had made them look like a bunch of leering peasants, he complained. Customers were there to be respected, not lampooned, he said.

It was my first but not my last experience of the pains of reconciling an artistic eye with the sensitivities of commerce.

* * *

And all this explains my choice of *Sarratt?* You ask.

Well, yes, as a matter of fact, in a tortuous way I really think it does. Dick is very much a man of the countryside, and he was still without Sarah and Micklefield Hall to go home to in the evenings. So when the working day ended, neither of us could wait to pile into his Roadster and take to the open Hertfordshire landscape. For him, it was an escape from the town, for me a blessed easing of the day's humiliations. I had no earthly idea what career I would follow when I was grown up. I didn't even realise there was no such thing as being grown up. Coasting through the still unspoiled country lanes, I looked around me restlessly for a world I could inhabit. It never occurred to me that the only sure way to find such a world was to invent one.

Thus Sarratt, as we passed through it on our way to nowhere in particular, impressed itself upon me as some kind of secret haven, a forgotten piece of real England just round the corner from subtopia. And because I am an incurable house-fantasiser, I imagined myself living there in some context

18

still to be defined, at the edge of the real world but safe from it.

And it is no wonder to me at all that when twenty years later I came to select a birthplace for my secret England, I should have lighted upon Sarratt's pretty village green and cosy redbrick cottages and half-hidden mansions and Sarratt's exquisitely beautiful Church of the Holy Cross, and imagined them as the keepers of an English mystery of which I was some kind of undefined inheritor.

So I called my training school the Nursery. And I put it in Sarratt where I had once longed to live. In the world of George Smiley and his people, after all, there is no place more dangerous than home.

* * *

What became of me after the Summer Sales is predictable. I returned to Oxford, went on to teach, played in secret England for a while, then went to the Devil and became a writer.

What became of Dick is worth recording because, unlike our modern spies, many of his achievements remain unsung. As a fully paid-up closet rebel he became, of course, a magistrate, a High Sheriff and a person of immense if occasionally subversive respectability. He now lords it over a spirited family and a great house, but humanity and self-mockery deprive him of pomp. He spends much of his leisure time on the operating- table while surgeons strive to correct the Sydney Bridge effect in later age. So far he has to his credit half-a-dozen hip replacements, three to each side, and a complicated spine operation to keep the central struts relatively upright.

More recently, surgeons had the temerity to tamper with his heart. Dick, who likes to pretend he is a skinflint, probably maintains they couldn't find it. More objective reports suggest that it is as big as ever.

Apart from these minor infringements of his liberty, Dick Edmonds is what he always was: a cussed, crabby, amusing, loyal, witty, idiosyncratic, deeply affectionate friend, too droll, too self-aware, too old and wise from birth, too sad at heart, ever to desert the common lot.

Oh, and I did finally pay off the charcoal suit.

Mikhail Lyubimov

Mikhail Lyubimov, a close friend of Kim Philby, who contributed to the recently published The Private Life of Kim Philby – The Moscow Years, *was born in 1934, graduated at The Moscow State Institute of International Relations and became a KGB Intelligence Officer in 1958. He served in the Soviet Embassy in Helsinki 1958/59, London from 1961 until expelled in 1965 and finally in Copenhagen 1967 – 1980.*

He resigned from the KGB in 1980. Subsequently he has pursued a successful career as a writer of books and plays as well as being a frequent broadcaster and commentator. He lives in Moscow with his third wife Tatiana.

THE ADVENTURES OF COLONEL KARLA IN SARRATT
Translated by Natasha Franklin

On this particular Saturday morning it was deceptively tranquil in Kensington Palace Gardens, or Millionaires' Row as it is also known, where the Soviet Embassy is located. Only the leaves were rustling under the breath of a light breeze drifting over from Kensington Palace. However, I knew full well that the MI5 surveillance squads had traced my every step from where I lived on Porchester Terrace to the Embassy building. The entire street was stuffed with hidden television cameras and even the iron gate leading into the neighbouring Kensington Gardens was monitored.

I went into the building slowly, climbed the staircase and entered the KGB residence, opening the door with a special key. Hardly had I walked in, when my back began to ache; to all intents and purposes we worked in an electrified iron sack, protected from infra-red and other rays, directed at the premises by the British counter-intelligence for bugging purposes. The windows were covered with armour-plated shutters. We were strictly forbidden to open them; several air conditioners churned cold air around and all the spies frequently caught colds as a result. There was no respite anywhere. You did not even get a break from vigilance in the loo; several times MI5 had put sensitive bugging equipment made of plastic in the sewer pipes and it was possible to hear colleagues' conversations in the corridor through them.

How I envied those Englishmen, who used go out to the countryside at weekends on picnics or to their cottages! How lucky they were to get the chance to enjoy nature! Alas, for us KGB intelligence officers, Saturdays and Sundays were the busiest days; firstly, Moscow loved to offload a batch of tasks at the end of the week. That could mean a flight to Accra for a secret meeting with a leader of a national liberation movement and the public burning of the American president in effigy as a sign of protest against the latest intervention, the urgent redeployment of the Embassy's driver, whom the Ambassador had by chance found in bed with his wife, or the purchase for comrade Brezhnev of a state-of-the-art hunting rifle. Secondly, at the weekends the powerful surveillance squads would slacken off slightly and we would make the most of this English peculiarity to carry out operations. The weekend for the Englishman was as holy as a cup of tea at four o'clock or a pint of beer in a favourite pub in the evening.

21

My back was still aching. I opened the fridge bar, took out a bottle of vodka, drank a couple of large shots and called the cipher clerk. My head started to buzz a little, but the pain in my back subsided and I was seized with a wild energy, capable of trampling all the secret objectives of the United Kingdom to dust. I drank a few more shots to calm down.

The cipher clerk placed a telegram on the table in front of me. It read: "Top Secret

To Colonel Karla:

You are ordered to carry out the excavation on Sunday evening of valuable materials from a dead letter box located by the western wall of the Church of the Holy Cross, Sarratt, Hertfordshire. The exact location: north two foot from the tomb of the Clutterbuck family, the traditional squires of the village. The documents have been placed there by our valued agent and it is your task to send them on to Moscow via the diplomatic bag. At the same time we would like you to gather full information about a certain Mr Edmonds who is supposedly a flourishing local businessmen but in actual fact is a dangerous agent of the Secret Intelligence Service who is conducting actively subversive work against the Soviet Union. Take particular care while carrying out this operation."

Below there was the general's signature and an attachment: a map of Sarratt and a plan pointing out the whereabouts of the cache.

Where was this Sarratt, damn it? Although while still at the Comrade Andropov Spy School, we learnt all the towns and villages of England by rote, this place had slipped my memory and I had to consult the reference book. It turned out that Sarratt was founded almost at the same time as Moscow – what a strange coincidence! Although at the time the inhabitants of Sarratt were totally unaware of even the existence of Russia and we knew nothing about the English. Meanwhile, the Grand Princes of Kiev at the time considered Paris a remote and filthy village, although, it's true, they had never paid Sarratt a visit!

Yet another Sunday ruined! All normal people are usually busy relaxing with their families, strolling in Hyde Park in old boots and tattered pullovers, spending the evening at striptease bars in Soho... The Soviet spy on the other hand does not get days off, he works round the clock in obscurity until he dies and then God forbid he receives a full military salute of honour at his grave.

I spent all day in the residence reading various telegrams. Towards evening I went home, having downed the rest of the bottle of vodka.

"What are you looking so agitated about, Karla?", my wife, Tatiana, asked tenderly. I merely wrinkled my brow at which she disappeared into the kitchen to prepare the haggis; recently I had put on weight and therefore asked her to make me dishes which would kill my appetite.

"We'll have to go down to the Portobello Road tomorrow to get some vegetables", I remarked as if incidentally. But my experienced wife, who had taken special courses in the KGB, immediately understood without further explanation that an operation had been assigned for tomorrow. And in any case what explanations could there be, if my entire flat was littered with bloody MI5 bugs. What could I say if there was an invisible little hole in the bedroom ceiling through which counter-intelligence recorded my every move right down to my facial expressions. All this was extremely irritating, especially when my wife and I were alone in our bedroom. And what could I do – remove all the bugs or stop up the hole? They would only insert new ones. To hell with the lot of them!

Sunday morning. Hateful haggis; it dampens the desire not only to eat but also to carrying on living. I lay slumped on the sofa, flicking through the newspaper and marvelling at what one can write about in a country where nothing interesting ever happens; no revolutions, no perestroikas and every morning the milkman leaves a pint of milk by the front door. What monotony!

But it was time to get going. I flung on a tweed jacket, corduroy trousers and sporting shoes, like a true English gentleman. We took big shopping bags with us and waved them around as we moved towards the car in the happy knowledge that our neighbour upstairs, an MI5 agent, had already noticed the bags and was informing someone by telephone that we were heading for Portobello market. My wife got in behind the wheel of my battered Ford (security rules! Why risk standing out? Yet I could easily have bought a Rolls Royce!) and we set off for the market.

In the Portobello Road, I could genuinely relax; this was not one of these soulless scenes one finds at the Tate or the National Gallery. Here life was in full swing in all its brilliant colours. We wandered around the market for a whole hour, picking up potatoes, cabbage, my favourite "grannies" and grapes. We chucked everything into the boot and from here the important business began; from the Portobello Road we drove onto Ladbroke Grove and crossed under the railway line. This meant that if someone was following us then their car would be forced to get on our tail, providing, of course, that MI5 had still not invented a car à la James Bond, which could fly across railway tracks or become invisible. Nobody was behind us but we were not going to relax. We took a left turn, then a right, jumped a red light (almost knocking down an old lady at the zebra crossing!), turned left again and then took another right. My wife who was looking intensely in the mirror, winked at me; there was no one on our tail! We took a right turn and I leapt out of the practically still moving vehicle and ran into a pub, while my wife sped straight off. Even if the surveillance squads had driven over the railway tracks, they would not have been able to see me leaping out of the car... See you later, Tatiana!

I drank half a pint of Guinness in the pub, walked out onto the street, grabbed a taxi and continued my surveillance. At Preston Road tube I asked the driver to stop. Thank God, no one was around. I sat down in the last carriage on the tube train and went as far as Croxley. Here I noticed a few suits on the platform and I travelled back in the opposite direction. So far there was nothing suspicious, there was no surveillance. Just to be on the safe side I got out at Moor Park and went the rest of the way to Rickmansworth on foot. Sarratt was nearby now, damn it! God, I was tired! Damnable work for lunatics! Once in Rickmansworth I took another taxi and reached Sarratt, asking the driver to drop me at the bottom of North Hill by the bridge over the river.

Quiet flowed the marvellous stream of the Chess and there were water meadows, wood violets, primroses and wood anemones. Ducks paddled around serenely and there was even a pair of white swans. What a place this would be to settle in old age, tend roses, go fishing, recalling from time to time a glorious past of espionage. It could not be more different from Moscow with its eternal frosts and snow. Why did God insult us with such a climate?

I walked across the fields and up the hill straight to Holy Cross Church, the location for my task. I caught sight of the iron railing along the eastern part of the wall immediately. The Clutterbuck family tomb where I would find the dead letter box was behind the railing. It was far too public a place and I would only be able to carry out my task in the dark.

It was still not dark, however, and to chat to anyone here would be dangerous; the English, like the Chinese, are a suspicious bunch and any stranger attracts attention. I walked into The Cock Inn and ordered a double scotch. I tried not to speak; God forbid the barman suspecting me of being a foreigner! What on earth could a foreigner be doing in such a parochial spot as Sarratt?

I drank the whisky slowly, paid and went outside. It was already dark and there was not a soul to be seen. The local inhabitants were probably all ensconced in their little burrows in front of the television. In our country only the old women do this, while the men are out distilling home-made vodka and downing bottles until they crash out.

Stealthily, I approached the fence around the grave and tried to open the gate. It was locked, damn it! What was I to do? But as comrade Stalin used to say, there are no fortresses that the Bolsheviks cannot storm. I mulled over this problem for an instant then, with a desperate effort, hauled myself up onto the fence, like an orang-utan. Feeling smug, I jumped down elegantly. With horror I heard a ripping sound. It was my trousers! A spike on the railing had caught them in the waistband and ripped them apart! God, now I was left standing in my underpants. If only my subordinates could see their colonel now! But work must always come first. As Rudyard Kipling wrote in his *Spies' March*: "We march with colours furled, only concerned when Death breaks loose on a front of half the world."

Well, I had reached my goal. I swivelled my head round and saw that I was right next to the family tomb. But not the Clutterbuck tomb! Clearly written was the name "Ralph Day", whose family, I discovered later were, 150 years ago, keen rivals to the Clutterbucks in the squirearchy of Sarratt. Those stupid idiots holed up in Moscow! Could they not have checked? But then again a glance at my briefing note made me realise it was I who was wrong. The dead letter box was to the west of the Church not to the East as I supposed. My mistake – even more irritating! Here I should confess a weakness; I am terrified of cemeteries as I am of fire.

In cemeteries strange things happen to me including even sudden fainting fits. And it's a terrible fear to have, because all intelligence services love to make use of cemeteries not only for dead letter boxes, but also for rendezvous. Who is going to be suspicious of a two mournful looking people paying their respects at a grave? Very recently after placing a wreath at the graveside of Karl Marx in Highgate Cemetery in London, I started to wander back along the path towards the exit when all of a sudden I saw Marx himself walking towards me! I reasoned that I was hallucinating but when he drew level with me, he leaned over slightly, and tickled me with his enormous beard. The shock caused me to fall over.

But to work! I crept around the churchyard and luck being with me I soon found the imposing Clutterbuck tomb. I got out my compass and measured two foot from the grave to the north. I took a fold-up portable spade out of my bag (a £200 Samsonite procured at Harrods, incidentally) and suddenly spotted two huge blazing eyes which were more terrifying even than the infamous hound of the Baskervilles. Don't tell me it was Marx again? God, for a moment fear froze me to the spot; my entire body was dripping in sweat. The eyes were boring into me like green searchlights.

I quickly took control of myself – call yourself a Soviet spy! I raised the spade up in a threatening gesture, the eyes started to quiver, and I could hear a rustle in the bush and in the light of the moon I could see a fat cat making off. What was a cat doing in a cemetery anyway? Weren't its owners feeding it its favourite Whiskas so that it was compelled to hunt for dead people's bones? This little adventure cheered me up and I automatically reached for the back pocket of my torn trousers where I keep my whisky flask and quickly drew from it a generous gulp.

"What are you doing here?"

I started with a nervous cough. Standing right in front of me was a priest holding a small torch in his hand. He was a nice looking chap of about fifty-five but wearing a look of intense indignation.

"What right do you have to trespass in here without permission? What cheek! I shall call the police immediately."

"Forgive me, padre, I'm here for personal reasons. A relative of mine is buried here..."

"What do you mean, relative? Only the Clutterbucks are buried here!

And why are you talking with a foreign accent? Are you a spy or something?", and he shone the torch in my face.

"I'm a Pole, padre, but I have lived in London all my life. My father emigrated from Poland during the war. He served in the army under General Anders and fought against the Germans and then against the Russians. An extraordinary event occurred... allow me to explain..."

At this point the torch found my pants and my ripped trousers and the vicar's face softened.

"Come on, let's go into the church. It's not the done thing here to race around the cemetery half naked... Are you a Catholic?"

"Of course, Father – I mean padre! But I have got so used to the Church of England that, unfortunately, I very rarely follow strictly Catholic services", I said in agitation gazing sycophantically into the vicar's eyes.

We went into the church through the back entrance and through to a pokey little room.

"Here's a needle and thread for you", he said. "You can repair your trousers. What were you doing by the grave anyway?"

I explained somewhat incoherently that my invalid uncle had asked me to come here on his dead father's birthday and to place a candle right next to the grave in honour of him. Evidently, I had got confused somewhere along the way and come to the wrong place... Everything sounded so improbable that the vicar clearly took me for an idiot. As soon as I could, I pulled on my now carelessly repaired cords and started to look almost like a gentleman again.

"The Clutterbucks' used to live in Micklefield Hall, where Mr Edmonds now lives. Perhaps your uncle is acquainted with him?"

That surname pierced through me like an arrow. God, what luck! But I did not let on that it was familiar to me.

"Dear padre", I said, smiling like a Cheshire cat, "Would you drink a little whisky with me in memory of the deceased, buried somewhere here?"

He hesitated, but he was generally an agreeable fellow. It occurred to me that perhaps I should recruit him. The KGB was always in need of priests. Firstly, they could give a lot of interesting information about the people they take confessions from, especially from the ranks of the Foreign Office and the Conservative Party. Secondly, the KGB needed the church records where births and deaths were registered. I remember many years ago receiving a passport, having produced a birth certificate, which we obtained through our agent, a priest. The person I was claiming to be had actually been dead for some time. The police checked the date of birth against the parish register and gave me a real passport without any problem. A good priest is a real find for a spy. But now was not the time for taking on new recruits.

"So, padre, shall we have a little tipple?"

He found some glasses and I poured from my hip flask and surreptitiously slipped a pill into his glass. The tablet affects even the strongest of people and soon knocks them out.

"Who exactly is Mr Edmonds?", I asked with a smile.

"Oh, he's a real character!" The priest was ready to tell me everything that he knew and I had better steer him in the right direction.

"He doesn't by any chance work in the Secret Intelligence Service?"

"It would be odd if he didn't work in that venerable institution", the vicar said amicably.

"Does he have any weaknesses? Is there anything compromising?"

"He's a member of a large prestigious family. He is a great lover of shooting and fishing, he goes skiing... In general he is a real bon viveur!"

(I'll say! In MI6, just as in the KGB they were virtually all bon viveurs. Otherwise what would be the point in spying?)

"Nevertheless, does he have any weaknesses?", I ventured brazenly.

"If he has one weakness, it's that he's as strong as an ox!", the priest joked, gradually dropping off and lowering his head onto the table.

Not wanting to lose time, I went outside. There was a deathly silence and my nerves began playing up again. The ruddy cemetery! As long as no one leapt up out of the grave as they did in the stories of Edgar Allan Poe. My nerves had started to run riot; clearly I watched far too many horror films on television.

I was once again at the dead letter box. According to the description, the container was to look like a big stone. I retrieved my spade and began digging. Everything was quiet, the reverend father was asleep and, I hoped, would eventually wake up. I sat down on the ground and suddenly my hand felt something slimy. God, not again! I gave a yelp of terror, but luckily it was not a poisonous snake but a large frog. My forehead was once again dripping with sweat, I would have to pay the doctor a visit as my nerves were in shreds. I started digging again. The spade struck against the stone and I broke up the loose earth with my hands, pulled out the stone and shoved it in my Samsonite. This was my container with the materials.

The deed was done and now I could not afford to lose a minute. I pressed my signal button and five minutes later my Ford with Tatiana at the wheel drove up to the church. She had been waiting for me in a lane for some hours already and listening out for the signal. My wife was the pride of not only me but also the entire KGB (and not, I hope, the boss's lover) and she had been awarded a sabre with a special inscription for her services in battle.

We hurtled back to London and rushed back into our cosy little abode at Porchester Terrace. Now we had to open the container, take out the materials and prepare them to be sent on in the diplomatic bag. It was strange but the essential button on the plaster cast of the stone was missing. I opened it under the table to prevent MI5 seeing me through the hole in the ceiling. I struck the rock with a heavy blow of the hammer and it split open. And there in front of me lay a small box with the inscription "Edmonds". I opened it carefully. I must be hallucinating! There were no documents inside the box, but instead brilliant diamonds! There were about twenty of them, and furthermore they were clearly antique.

"Tanya, come here!", I called huskily.

Tatiana bent down beneath the table and nearly fainted from happiness.

"My dear Karla! Those are real gems! There are enough there to last the rest of our lives! God, how I love you!"

We found out later that the dead letter box with the secret materials was in a different cemetery and that the KGB had managed to get everything muddled up, something which happens very regularly in secret services. Naturally, I did not race back to Sarratt to return the treasure. Moreover, we gave a chunk of it to the KGB who do all sorts of wonderful things for the benefit of peace and all humankind!

But every time Tatiana and I sit down to drink our vodka, we always toast the venerable Dick Edmonds, the man responsible for making us rich.

William Petre

William Petre is the author of several published histories, including The Dana Story *and* Navigating the Century. *He is also a frequent contributor to a wide range of newspapers, magazines and specialist journals. A Londoner but currently based in Hertfordshire, he loves to travel all over the world – particularly when he has editors after him pestering him to meet a deadline.*

There were three cars in the convoy. They were driving too fast and too close down the narrow wooded lane, but they were sleek and new and they made so little noise I didn't hear them until it was too late. I was going far too fast myself, pedalling hard down the steep hill to get up speed for the rise on the far side, when the first car, a blue Cavalier, whipped the corner into my view. I swerved left to avoid it but I hit the grassy bank and rebounded back into the roadway as it flashed past. Out of control, there was no way I could avoid the second car, a huge silver Bentley already screeching its brakes. I slammed violently against the bumper, and was thrown headlong onto the bonnet. My forehead cracked on the tinted windscreen and for a moment my face pressed up against it.

And just a few inches away on the other side of the glass, like a distorting mirror, a face stared back into mine – a passenger hurtled forward by the speed of the Bentley's braking. We locked eyes for a bare moment, just long enough for me to notice his expression and the unnatural whiteness in his skin.

He looked terrified.

For a moment, still disoriented, I was gratified that he was so concerned on my behalf; but then I recognised who it was and even as his face snatched away, I realised that he wasn't frightened for me; but of me.

He must have thought I was some kind of KGB hitman, come for him before he could talk.

There was a grinding screech behind me as the Cavalier reversed hard back up the lane. Car doors opened all around me. I turned onto my back to see two men in loud tweed suits approaching, their hands reaching inside the breasts of their suits even as I watched. They pulled out handguns and pointed them at me and I swear they were ready to shoot.

I lay on my back on the bonnet, stretched my hands slow as snails up the glass, then kept absolutely still.

"It's okay," shouted one of the men to his colleague. "It's okay. I know him. It's only Ray. He works up at the Nursery."

I recognised his voice. Peter Frayne. Not my favourite person, but I can tell you I was pleased to see him.

His colleague frowned in surprise. "He's one of us?"

"*Him?*" laughed Frayne in derision. "No. He's an odd-job man. Isn't that right, Ray. You fix lights and things?"

I could barely speak, so I nodded.

"Listen, Ray," said Frayne. "You've signed the act, right?"

"Yes."

Frayne waved his gun-hand to indicate the road, the cars, the fat grey man inside. "Then this never happened. You never saw us. You understand?"

"Yes."

"Good." Frayne touched the muzzle of his gun to his lips, then holstered it. He was smiling now, cocky, back in control. He reached out a hand and hauled me off the bonnet to my feet. With one more meaningful look, he and his companion returned to their Cavalier. Dizzily, I picked my bike off the lane and dragged it to the side of the road to let the Bentley and a second Cavalier pass. I watched the cars drive away up the hill until they turned out of sight. Thirty seconds later I saw them flickering through the branches of leafless trees, back in close convoy, driving up the lane to the Nursery.

Where else?

* * *

The Cock was busy for a Tuesday. Sue was serving Ken and his lady, while the two Mikes were on their regular stools by the bar. I said good evening to them as I bought myself a beer, but they were locked in their own talk, as usual. They didn't object to me, but they didn't make any effort to include me, either.

Most of the noise was coming from two tables pushed together where the dartboard used to be. I could see Shane's back and Old Paulie and Alf and Claire, but there was also a woman sitting by Shane I didn't immediately recognise. I nodded to the two Mikes then took my beer over to their table.

The woman was young, no more than twenty-five. I'd never seen her before. I'd have remembered. She was stylish, well groomed, with angelic features and long fair hair falling forward off her shoulders. But the thing

I noticed most were her hazel eyes; wide and shy and innocent, staring out at me like a young child from behind a window.

"Ray, mate," said Shane from beside me, his voice high on alcohol and new friendship. "This is Katrina. She's just moved to Chandler's Cross."

"So *you* are Ray," she said, offering me her hand across the table. "Your friends have been talking about you."

I took and shook her hand while still I held her eyes, and Christ! It was like opening a door into a gale. She felt something too. I know she did. Her eyes flickered in startlement and looked away. She hurriedly withdrew her hand.

I said to her: "And what exactly were they saying?"

"I was telling her about the Nursery," said Shane, animatedly.

"You what?" I exclaimed, darting Shane a fierce look.

"C'mon," protested Shane. "Everybody knows."

"With *your* damned mouth." But he had a point. Everyone in Sarratt knew about the Nursery, although we rarely talked about it. I'd known about it myself since I was seven or eight. They couldn't hope to hide it completely from the locals, and they knew it. One of them told me once it was like acne; after a point, the harder you tried to conceal it, the more attention you drew. And so their security was light but effective. Even I didn't know most of what went on inside.

"So what is so secret about this place?" asked Katrina.

"Let's talk about something else, eh."

Katrina leaned across the table. "Come on," she coaxed. "Just one little secret. There must be something you can tell us that won't jeopardise the safety of the Western world."

"Please," I asked. "Don't press me. I'm not allowed."

"You never say a damned word," muttered Old Paulie. "Making yourself out to be so important."

"Have you got all the gadgets?" asked Shane, facetiously. "Exploding cigarettes and that? Maybe your bicycle has got one of them ejector seats?"

"It did today," I laughed.

"How do you mean?" asked Katrina.

"Never mind," I replied, quickly. "It was nothing."

"Come on," said Katrina. "You have to tell us *something*."

33

"I'll tell you this," I said, truthfully. "I have a routine job that has nothing to do with anything you'd find interesting."

"That's what all spies say," she laughed. "That's what spies are *supposed* to say! It's true! You really *are* a spy!"

"Yeah," muttered Old Paulie. "Double O zero."

"Don't be like that," piped up Claire in my defence. "It's not his fault he's not allowed to talk."

"Well Christ!" said Old Paulie. "He's making himself out to be all this, but he's just a bleeding electrician! He changes their bleeding fuses, is all he does."

"How do you know what he does?"

Katrina leaned forward right at that moment, with my attention distracted, and asked: "What about this Russian, then? What about him?"

I must have looked a fool. I could feel my mouth drop open and I spilled half my pint onto the table. I looked into her eyes but they had turned to marble and I couldn't read anything behind them. She smiled, softened, the moment passed, and Sue came clucking over with a towel to soak up the mess. The conversation finally switched away from the Nursery and I was happy to forget about it.

More fool me.

* * *

I bumped into Frayne next day at the Nursery. He was with a small, rumpled man in a faded grey suit. It was almost like they'd been looking for me, because the man stepped across my path. He had a good, warm smile on him, but I didn't believe a bit of it.

"You must be Ray Hurst," he said.

"Yes sir. And you are?"

"Oliver Adams," he replied, in the familiar, offhand way that told me he was lying and didn't care that I knew. "I understand you've applied to join us."

"*Him?*" interjected Frayne, incredulously. "Joining *us?*"

"It was Mr Rodgers' idea, sir," I explained. "With him retiring next month, sir, and his position open."

34

"But…"

"Is there something wrong?" frowned Adams. "Do you know any reason he *shouldn't* join us?"

"I've never heard anything so ridiculous," said Frayne, testily.

"With respect, sir," I said, addressing both, "I believe I can look after the maintenance of this building as well as anyone. I already do it when Mr Rodgers is away. And that's almost three days out of five."

"That's not the point," snapped Frayne. "This is a Civil Service position. You're not in the Civil Service."

"It never used to be," I replied. "It wasn't Civil Service before Rodgers, and they only gave it to Rodgers to keep him busy until he retired, not because it needs him."

"What I mean is," explained Frayne, "there are security considerations."

"What you mean," I retorted, "is you don't trust me because I haven't been to one of your precious schools, or Oxbridge or Sandhurst or wherever."

Adams laughed warmly, clapped me on the shoulder. "Well spoken, Mr Hurst. I believe that's exactly what he means." He closed the door, then ushered Frayne and me into chairs. For all his easy charm, Adams had real authority about him. I found myself feeling far more wary of him than I was of Frayne.

"I wanted to talk about something else as well," said Adams, to me. "Mr. Frayne said you saw our guest arriving yesterday."

"Yes."

"And you know who he is?"

"Yes."

"You haven't mentioned this to anyone?"

"Of course not!" I replied, shocked.

"Good. You know, that makes you one of only fourteen people in the whole world who know where he is. The Russians would give a fortune to know what you know. It won't matter after tomorrow, because we're moving him first thing, but until then, I'd rather you kept it to yourself. Completely. Understood?"

"Yes sir."

* * *

I stayed home that night. I made myself a stiff drink and wandered restlessly around the cottage. It was about eight when there was a knock on my front door. I didn't get many visitors, but every so often someone would try to flog me tea-towels or salvage my soul, and my mind was so distracted I opened the door without a thought.

"Katrina!" I exclaimed. "What the… What are you doing here?"

"I hope you don't mind," she said. "I got your address from the directory."

"No. No. Come in. Come in. You want a drink?"

Katrina took my glass from me, sipped it and grimaced. "Ugh! What is that?"

"Whisky and water."

"Anything but that."

I led her to my kitchen, showed her the inside of my fridge. She picked out a carton of apple juice while I washed and handed her a glass.

"You must think me very forward," she said. "But really, we got on so well last night I knew you wouldn't mind."

"I don't." I led her back into the sitting room and sat at one end of the sofa.

Katrina sat beside me. "Shyness is a strange thing," she said. "I'm usually very shy, but with some people I never feel shy at all. I feel at home with them from the first moment. Do you feel that way?"

"Yes," I said.

"I felt that way with you," she said.

My heart gave a little hammer.

"Didn't you feel that way?" she asked.

"Yes," I told her. "I did."

She smiled broadly. "Come on then. Do I have to do everything? Aren't you going to ask me out to dinner or something?"

"I don't have a car."

"We'll take mine."

"I can't," I said, nervously drinking my whisky. "Not tonight. Maybe tomorrow?" It was then that I started to feel strange. My head felt dizzy and my stomach sick and my limbs heavy. I glanced down at my empty

36

glass, then across at Katrina. She reached across and took my glass from my hand and I knew instantly that she had spiked my drink. I tried to stand up but I couldn't. I slumped forward into blackness. I don't remember anything else.

* * *

I woke up while it was still dark outside, stretched out on my sofa. My head hurt as if it had been ripped open, but my memory came back with a jolt as I remembered how Katrina had called in and how I had blacked out. I rolled off the sofa onto my knees and almost instantly made the connection between Katrina and the Russian at Sarratt. I remembered Adams saying how the KGB would do anything to stop him talking.

Then I remembered Adams saying he was moving the Russian first thing this morning.

I grabbed my phone but the line was dead. I didn't wait but ran headlong out of my cottage. My bike was still broken and there was no traffic around, so I ran all the way to Sarratt. I ran with my heart pounding and the fear of disaster in my mind. I didn't know how it all fitted together, but I knew I had to warn Adams. I knew I had to stop the transfer.

I was too late.

It all happened right in front of me. Framed by the rising sun, I saw the silver Bentley coming down the lane, fronted and backed up by Cavaliers. The convoy reached the end of the lane, turned towards me. Instantly, there was shouting from the woods to my left followed by gunfire. The Bentley's windows shattered and glass sprayed everywhere as it ploughed into the bank.

Both Cavalier's screeched to a halt and Frayne leapt out of the passenger seat of the first. He drew his gun and ran over to the Bentley and threw open the back door. From where I was, I could see there was no-one inside.

Soldiers in camouflaged uniforms emerged abruptly from the woods on both sides. They held two men between them and jostled them over to the leading Cavalier.

Frayne looked bewildered. He was wandering around with his gun out and an expression of anxious bewilderment. He saw me and his sense of purpose instantly returned. "Traitor," he cried, striding towards me. "You filthy traitor." He pointed his gun at my chest and his finger was tightening on the trigger when Adams appeared from nowhere and slapped away his hand.

"What in Hell's name do you think you're doing?" demanded Adams. "Are you mad?"

"It was him. Someone tipped off the Russians. It had to be him."

I tried to protest but I was still too winded from my run. "I've… I've done nothing," I gasped, finally. "I ran all the way here to warn you."

"Then you're admitting you knew," said Frayne, pointing savagely. "He's admitting it."

"No," I protested. I was about to tell them all about Katrina, but I trailed off. I didn't know her part in all this, but I knew for certain I wouldn't give her up to Frayne and Adams and their methods. "What are you accusing me of? I didn't even know anything."

Adams took me by the arm. "We've known there was a leak at the Nursery for months," he said. "We narrowed the source to one of five people, including you. All the information came from areas to which you had access. Then, after you ran into our guest, two Russian embassy staff that we like to keep an eye on were seen in this area, a woman and a…"

"What's that got to do with me?"

"The old marked fiver trick," said Adams. "I told you we were moving our guest at dawn. *Only* you. And then this happens."

"But I wasn't the only one to know," I pointed out. "You were there."

"Yes," said Adams. "So I was. But *I* didn't tell anyone."

"And Frayne was there," I reminded him.

Frayne laughed. "Don't even try to bring me into this?"

"He has a point," said Adams, calmly. "After all, you were on our list, too."

"*Me*! Don't be ridiculous. You told me yourself I was ruled out."

"I lied," said Adams, softly, his smile barely detectable. And I knew in that instant exactly what was going on. Frayne realised it too. His eyes went wide and I saw his gun begin to lift even as he assessed his situation, head-counting the soldiers around him.

38

"Don't even think about it, Frayne," said Adams. "It's over. You're under arrest."

"No." Now he did raise his handgun, pointed it at Adams. "Never."

"Put it away," chided Adams. "We removed the pin long before we let you come into contact with our guest."

But Frayne kept pointing it at Adams anyway, hand trembling. He pulled the trigger futilely twice before a soldier stepped forward and seized his wrist, twisted the gun from it so violently that it skittered along the tarmac. I saw tears spring to Frayne's eyes, and I couldn't tell whether it was pain or self-pity. A moment later he was being led away.

"A dangerous thing, vanity," commented Adams, as we watched. "People talk about spies being motivated by political beliefs and greed and idealism and all kinds of things. But with people like Frayne, the thing that motivates them is no more than self-importance."

"I don't understand," I interrupted. "How *did* you know it wasn't me?"

"We never for a moment thought it was you," laughed Adams. "You didn't have either the access or the profile. But you made for a good decoy to lull Frayne. I made doubly certain last night. I had one of my people follow you home, cut your telephone wires, then put you out of commission. You were supposed to be unconscious all morning."

"One of *your* people? *Katrina?*"

"Yes." He turned to the second Cavalier, beckoned. The back door opened, Katrina stepped out, walked across to us.

Adams nodded at her: "You two know each other, I believe."

I could barely speak. "I don't..."

"Katrina is one of my finest vetting officers. You can understand, it's our policy to vet people we are considering employing. We were checking you out anyway, then when you bumped into our guest, we decided to act at once."

"I don't believe it."

"Don't hold it against her," said Adams. "It's her job. She does it exceptionally well, and besides, she gave you an excellent report." He allowed himself a small, dry smile. "A little too excellent, in truth." He stretched out his hand for mine. "Welcome aboard," he said.

Kurt Willinger

Kurt Willinger grew up in Brooklyn, New York, where he attended Brooklyn Technical High School and City College. He served in the US Air Force as a crew chief of fighter jets. After the service he worked as an aircraft mechanic for Pan American World Airways while completing his education.

He then pursued a career in advertising working first as a copywriter and eventually becoming the Creative Director and Vice Chairman of Saatchi & Saatchi Advertising worldwide.

Kurt is the recipient of numerous industry awards including CLIO's and the coveted grand prize at the Cannes Film Festival, the Lion d'or.

Currently Kurt actively pursues a literary career. His previously published works include a novel, The Spy in a Catcher's Mask, *and a pictorial history,* The American Jeep in Peace and War.

He and his wife, Doris, currently reside in Connecticut and devote their leisure time to travel and meddling in the lives of their three grown sons.

The contents of Peggy's jewellery box were reverently laid out on the red damask tablecloth. Surprising how many things she had accumulated over the years. The kids made their selections in turn. Leslie, the eldest, chose first, then Patty, Matthew, Susan and Jerry. It seemed to be the best way to distribute Peggy's treasures. When there were just a few items left I noticed the bracelet. It looked tarnished and forlorn. I picked it up.

"If you don't mind, kids, I'm keeping this."

I slipped it into my pocket. I'd forgotten that bracelet existed. This is our first family gathering since the funeral and it's nice to hear friendly noises in the old house. They think I'm handling their mother's passing well. I am not. I'm more angry than sad. I seem to wake up angrier every morning.

* * *

Peggy was wearing the bracelet the first time I saw her. It was at the dance at the Bovingdon enlisted club. They trucked in girls from surrounding towns. Watford, Hemel Hempstead, Chipperfield and Sarratt. "Suitable" girls from proper families according to the Red Cross. I remember thinking, how much fun could that be? I was in the Army Air Corps. Waist gunner on a B-17. That was over fifty-five years ago. I was just a kid, not yet twenty and very cocky. The Army and I didn't much see eye to eye back then. I ran a crap game and did a little business in after hours gasoline. They were always threatening to take my stripes away which, frankly, I could not care less. But I was a pretty fair gunner; had me two Me109's, and since without stripes you don't fly, we had us, what do you call it? A détente. Anyway, as the girls spilled into the club, us guys were giving them the once over. A couple were fat, one must have been six foot three, another had stick out teeth. We were cracking up.

"Hey, Bummie, lookit the keester on that one," my pal Augie nudged.

Everyone called me Bummie. I guess because I was from Brooklyn. Y'know, the Dodgers being the bums? In the midst of a rude cackle, I spotted Peggy. My mouth fell open but no sound emerged. I forgot to breathe. She had this face like a peach floating in sweet cream. Her big

41

eyes were taking in everything. She was smiling. But she wasn't smiling. That was the normal expression on her face. She was slim, kind of leggy, in a yellow print dress. Her light brown hair wasn't done up like some of the other girls. It sort of just framed her face like it grew that way. I started towards her but two guys were already talking to her. After waiting two impossibly long dance numbers, I made my move. "May I have the next dance, miss?" I heard my mouth say. A regular Ronald Colman. She looked me straight in the eye, smiled and said, "I'd be delighted." Her eyes flashed a kind of bottomless green which was tinged with purple. Her bracelet jingled as she took my arm. My knees turned to melted cheese at her touch. The band struck up a fast number. Oh, dammit, I was no jitterbugger. Fortunately, a couple of the guys were and we moved back in a circle to give them room. I kept hold of her hand as we watched the kids dance. They were good and she smiled in appreciation. Then she smiled at me. I had to say something. I couldn't think of anything. I heard her say, "So, where do you hail from, sergeant?" Wait. I know the answer to that. "Brooklyn. Brooklyn, New Yawk." And somehow we were having a conversation. Her name was Margaret Biggerstaff. She lived in Sarratt. She was nineteen. She had an older sister, Gwen, who was engaged to a Hurricane pilot. She thought Americans so interesting and fun-loving. "I'm Frank Davis." I didn't mention the Bummie nickname. Then the dance was over. "So nice to meet you, Sergeant Davis." Like a schmuck I mumbled thank you and turned to walk away. Something yanked me backwards. Her bracelet got itself snagged on my sleeve where the stripes were sewn on. Nearly tore those chevrons off. She said, "I'm terribly sorry," and by the time we got ourselves unhooked another number had started. She apologised again. And we both laughed. "Hey, Margaret, don't worry about it. I'm always losing my stripes." "Call me Peggy." "Peggy, that's a very unusual bracelet."

"It's my sister's. She lent it to me for the dance. My sister, Gwen. Did I mention I had a sister? You're in an aircrew? That's terribly dangerous, isn't it?"

"Nah, we got a great skipper. Terrific pilot." Listen to me. Suddenly I was a company man.

We had three more dances and I had to endure watching from

42

the sidelines for at least two dozen more before it was "Goodnight Sweetheart", the last dance.

"Hey, uh, you gonna be here for the next social?"

"Yes, Frank, I think so. But perhaps I should leave this bracelet at home."

"Heck no, Peggy. That's my lucky bracelet."

She laughed. She got it. I'm going to see her next week. In seven days, providing there's no mission. Jeez, I felt like I'm rolling nothing but sevens. I'm even considering not busting Master Sergeant Dumbrowski's chops tomorrow. Peggy showed up for the next dance. And the next. Once we even managed to dodge the chaperones and sneak outside for a walk. Strictly against the rules. We were back in a couple of minutes. I didn't want her to get into trouble. One standdown I biked into Bovingdon Village and phoned her at home. It was swell to hear her voice. I said I was coming to visit if it was okay with her. She said she'd meet me on Sarratt Village Green just near "The Boot". Can't miss it. I told her I'd be there. I knew I'd never make it on a bike so I copped a Jeep. She was waiting just where she said, on the Green, near the Boot. We walked. In the shade of a lime tree, I kissed her. We walked and talked some more. I kissed her again. This time she kissed me back. When I returned with the Jeep they nailed me. Misuse of government property. Restricted to barracks, pending. But the skipper bailed me out. We had an early mission and he didn't feel like breaking in a new gunner.

There was no dance the next weekend and I was hanging out on the ramp helping Krauss bleed *Miss Behavin's* brakes when some clown comes over and tells me he saw my girl get off a truck at the officer's club. I want to deck the guy but Augie nods his head and says, "Yeah, Bummie, I seen her too."

She's at the officer's dance? Sure, it figures. What would a swell dish like her want with a bum like me? Officers. That really eats me.

On our next mission everything went wrong. We got hit by flak over Regensberg and lost the formation. Then, with one engine feathered and another running rough, we were jumped by fighters who tore us up even more. We managed to limp to the Channel where we ditched the *Miss*. She was sinking fast and we had a heck of a time getting Samuels, the skipper, out before she went under. I had to climb up to the top of the fuselage and snake him out the side window. I got him loose just in time. Just as it was getting dark and I was promising myself that if I ever got out of this raft I was going to punch hell out of that officer, a rescue boat showed up. In no time we were warm and cosy in a Brighton hospital, slightly banged up but very happy to be alive.

For four days we are living the life of Riley. Good eats, free cigs, dishy nurses treating us like senators. But I can't help thinking about Peggy. Scheming broad. Really had me going there. I thought she really liked me. But then why should she like me; a mutt with nothing going for him.

The next morning the nurse tells me I've got a visitor. Me? A Miss Margaret Biggerstaff. I hurry out to the lounge and there she is. She looks happy to see me. "Oh, you're hurt," she says. My shoulder is heavily taped. "Nah, just sprained," I say. She gives me a very gentle hug but it feels like she really means it. She looks so beautiful, even with the worry on her face. She heard *Miss Behavin'* was missing. Then, that the crew was picked up in the Channel. She had to come to see me. Her boss at the store in Watford gave her the day off. We sit and talk. She holds my hand. Turns out her girlfriend didn't want to go to the officer's dance alone so she agreed to go with her. That's the kind of girl Peggy is.

I don't deserve this much luck. I'm happy listening to her talk, just looking at her. Even a Kraut buzz bomb was on my side. Just as visiting time was over, the sirens went off and everyone was herded to an inside hall. That gave me some more time with her. One nurse called it a Bob Hope bomb. She said when it flies over we just bob our heads and hope for the best. Funny, huh? You gotta hand it to those Brits, they got guts.

I decided right then that if I got close to finishing my missions I would ask Peggy to marry me. After my twenty-third, I asked her and she said "Yes" but I'd have to come home and meet her family to make it official. I would have rather faced the flak over Kassel. Nevertheless, I showed up. She lived in a neat flint cottage with a grey slate roof in Sarratt. Her Mom was nice and so was her sister, Gwen. Her Pop, who owned the Village garage and gas station was, on the other hand, none too cordial at first. I think the stuff I brought helped smooth the course. My buddy, Ernie, the mess sergeant, a fellow New Yorker, fixed me up with a whole ham, a leg of lamb, some butter, Hershey bars, a can of pineapple juice and a large can of pears. I asked Ernie if we might be overdoing it. He said, "trust me". When I pulled all the stuff out of my duffel, they just stood and stared like I had produced a piece of the true cross. Her Pop, who I made it a point to call 'sir', a lot, started to come around when I reached into the bottom of the bag and pulled out a box of cigars and a bottle of bourbon. I had used up all my favours in one shot but it was worth it. After dinner Peggy's old man took me aside and invited me to go for a walk. I was thinking he was going to kill me. We walked down the road not saying much, him smoking his pipe and me alert for any sudden move. When we got to the Cock, a pub opposite the church, he ordered two Scotch and sodas and took a corner table. I waited for him to speak. "To be perfectly honest, Mr. Davis, I'm against you and Maggie marrying. The times are so unsettled. There's a war going on, you know." I nodded. "Yes, sir. I know that." "But I know my daughter," he continued. "She's a headstrong girl and once she decides something, well that's it." He contemplated his whisky for a bit, then spoke again. "Well, she must see something in you. So, you have my blessing. Welcome to the family." He touched his glass to mine and that was that. Phew. Made my last mission seem like a stroll in the park.

We were married in Holy Cross Church in Sarratt. My CO, who would have loved to say no, had no choice but to give permission. I had three Nazi kills, flown my missions, and wore the Distinguished Flying Cross. I had paid my dues. Maggie came floating down the aisle looking like a storybook princess wearing a white wedding dress that was a gift from her boss at the store. Her sister, the maid of honour, made Peggy a present of the jingly bracelet. Both her Mom and my best man, Augie, were crying as the Vicar pronounced us man and wife.

Now that she's gone I can't imagine anything good every happening again. I keep her bracelet in my pocket but all it does is make a tinny sound.

* * *

Nearly a year has passed. The kids make their obligatory calls and

45

visits on the weekend. Then one Tuesday, Susan, the level-headed one, pays me an unexpected call. Lately I've been too weary to shave every day so I guess I looked fairly scruffy. It must have scared her. "You've got to do something Dad. Get out. Meet some people. You can't continue like this." I shrug. "Why not go on a cruise?" she suggests. "Get out of the house."

"Your mother and I went on a cruise a couple of times. We always had fun." Peggy made friends so easily. "I don't know. Without her...."

"So maybe a trip to Europe." She won't give up. "New surroundings." I'm shaking my head when she says, "Why not visit Mom's home town in England." I stop shaking my head. "Sarratt? Peggy's home? What would I do there?"

If Susan hadn't sent me the plane tickets and made all the reservations I probably wouldn't have come. But here I am at the Dorchester in London contemplating the route my rented Ford will take up the M1 to Watford and then through the country lanes to Sarratt.

In a short time I pass through Watford and notice that the store in which Peggy worked is still there and, from the looks of it, going strong.

It's not long before I arrive at Sarratt. Still a lovely little village. Houses built with brick and flint and well tended fences framing neatly cut lawns turned out in that special green that's so distinctly English. Everywhere too a blaze of daffodils proclaiming the season. This is the place that produced Peggy Biggerstaff. For which I will be eternally grateful.

I park the car in the centre of the Village and pull on my old corduroy jacket against the spring chill. Peggy's bracelet jingles in the side pocket. Before the trip, I asked a jeweller to fix up the bracelet. With undisguised disdain he declared that it wasn't worth the effort. I told him it was worth it to me. Now it looks shiny as new.

Disorientated, I walk along The Green in an effort to get my bearings. I'd been back to Sarratt several times with Peggy to show off the kids and attend funerals. But I'm still rather turned around. There are the two pubs, the Cricketers and the Boot. But I'm looking for the Cock. Then I remember. The Cock is in the direction of North Hill and the river. I head out on Church Lane. Strangely, I feel lighter than I've felt in some time. A few cars buzz by as I walk. I still can't get used to cars on the wrong side of the road. People pass and nod hello. Friendly people.

Then I see the church and the pub. I always thought it odd to find a church directly across from a tavern. The doorway to heaven so close to the entrance to the other place. I enter the Cock and order a pint. Sitting in the very corner where Peggy's dad and I sat so many years ago.

On the plane I resolved to visit the cemetery to find the Biggerstaff family plot. I considered leaving the bracelet on a stone or perhaps even burying it. Now that idea strikes me as a bit maudlin. The people I see seem to be enjoying life. I pay for the drink and decide to walk some more. A couple passes me. The young man is wearing jeans and a black jacket and pointy hair, the girl has at least five rings in each ear. But they seem happy together. Times change but people stay the same. Further up the road I encounter another young man walking with a girl. She's ten or eleven, most likely his daughter. She's got big eyes and skin colouring exactly like Peggy. Peaches and cream but with red hair. I nod to them. The man nods and says, "Hello." I stop, turn and say "Excuse me, I just found this bracelet in the road." The girl edges toward her father as I hold out the bracelet. "It must belong to some woman in town. I was wondering if you would take it and hold it until its rightful owner turns up."

Her father, a man in his mid-thirties, with light thinning hair, dressed in a running suit, eyes me sceptically. I introduce myself. "I'm Frank Davis. Just passing through. I hope you don't mind my imposing on your little girl. I'm leaving shortly and don't know who to give it to."

His expression softens and he nods to his daughter. "No, that's fine, right, Sophie?" Little Sophie looks at me, nods yes and then steps forward extending her hand. I drop the bracelet into it. "Thank you. You've taken a load off my mind." I say goodbye and turn away. I hear the little girl say goodbye. I turn to wave, then continue walking.

As I retrace my steps back to Sarratt Green, I feel better than I have in a long time. It occurs to me that bracelet has been looking after me for most of my life. It was time for it to take care of someone else.

I have all the time in the world to stroll around before heading back to London.

Mrs Eaves lay on her bed, eating a Mr Kipling's French Fancy and sulking.

Queenie was downstairs, ironing, seemingly oblivious to the fact that she was the cause of her boss's ill humour.

And it had all started off so well, thought Hermione irritably.

When Hermione Eaves had first heard that the filmstar Hugh Trent was renting out Little Sarratt Hall for the month of August, she was delighted. This was exactly the chance she'd been waiting for. When she caught wind of the rumours that he was cheating on his girlfriend with an unidentified lady, she was ecstatic. Now was the time to resurrect her career.

Knowing that Shirley, who helped out with the cleaning at Little Sarratt Hall, took her annual holiday in August, it didn't take long for Hermione to come up with a 3 point plan. Step 1: Go round to Little Sarratt Hall with the standard Welcome Pack of home-made fruit slices (Mr Kipling's). Step 2: Offer up the indispensable cleaning services of Queenie for a couple of morning's a week. Step 3: Sit back and wait for the exclusive, bi-weekly reports of the film star's private life (including lavish descriptions of the lover), whilst watching the smug smile disappear from Maureen Parker's face.

Steps 1 and 2 were completed – albeit with some difficulty due to Mr Trent's officious press secretary and her insistence on five different character references for Queenie. But Step 3 was proving problematic – chiefly due to Queenie's lamentable spying talents. After her first trip to the Hall, the only information she had managed to come up with was the fact that Mr Trent twisted himself into yogic poses for an hour each morning and ate only fruit before noon. The second report (delivered that morning) was no better – he slept in stripy pyjamas and kept *The Little Book of Calm* by his bedside.

Brushing off bits of icing from her cardigan and levering herself up from the bed, Hermione decided that a trip to the village shop was in order. But as soon as she entered Sarratt Stores, she wished she'd stayed at home. There in the queue, behind the tarty Donna Beggs, stood Maureen. Maureen the Hateful, who'd ruined her career. Maureen the Cuckoo, who'd so deviously ousted her from her carefully constructed nest.

Maureen the Usurper who'd stolen her crown.

It had all started with Maureen's May Day coup at the annual Sarratt Fair, when she'd caught the rather uptight Mrs Bambton round the back of The Boot in a drunken clinch with the man from the dodgems. Over the following 18 months, thanks to a steady succession of scoops, Maureen Parker had clawed her way up from village nobody to Sarratt's Number One Social Commentator. Leaving Hermione in her present position – obsolete.

Not for much longer, thought Hermione as she took her place in the queue behind Maureen.

"Hello, Mrs Eaves. Good weekend?"

"Lovely, thank you. And you?" Hermione knew what was coming next and immediately regretted her ill advised question.

"Super. Phil and Lisa were down with their two. I must say, grandchildren really are such fun. How's William? No nearer to settling down?" Hermione wondered briefly what Maureen's face would look like with no teeth.

"Well, he's still footloose and fancy free. But it's only a matter of time now."

"Is that right?" Maureen's tone suggested she wasn't entirely convinced.

Hermione glanced round, trying to think of another subject. An advert in the window caught her eye.

"Just look at what that strange, hippy woman, Sadie is offering: 'Reiki. Regression. Exploring your Chakras – I mean, whatever next?"

But Maureen was now talking to Donna and didn't appear to have heard.

Hermione's walk home was taken up primarily with thoughts of William. What was wrong him? Why couldn't he find a wife? He wasn't bad looking, He had a decent job as a senior marketing manager for Mr Kipling's, which was more than could be said for Maureen's son, who only scraped a living selling cameras in Watford High street.

By the time Hermione opened the front door, she was in quite a state. She went straight to the phone and rang her friend Anne, whose only daughter Sarah was also hopelessly single.

"Is Sarah coming down for the bank holiday?" There was no need to beat about the bush – both she and Anne spent enough time as it was, trying to matchmake their offspring.

"Probably. Why? Any brainwaves?"

"I was thinking that a little lunchtime drinks might be nice."

"Now that is a good idea. Who else should we invite?" Anne sounded excited already.

"The Stauntons, the Jenkins, the Rawlins... the usual crowd."

"But that means it will all be couples". Anne had an irritating habit of pointing out the obvious.

"Exactly. Then William and Sarah will start to feel the odd ones out and the penny might finally drop."

"Oh, you are clever" exclaimed Anne.

Walking into the kitchen for Monday's de-briefing session, Hermione found Queenie cramming a large piece of Chocolate Fudge Delight into her mouth, whilst studying one of her beloved safari brochures. Not for the first time, she wondered where she thought she'd get the money from to finance a trip to Kenya.

"When you've finished your mouthful, perhaps you'd like to tell me what you found out from your last trip to Little Sarratt Hall."

"Well". Queenie answered cagily. "Mr Trent doesn't like using the pool, apparently the chlorine's not good for his aura".

"That's it? That's all you managed to unearth in three hours?"

"Yes... but I saw something quite interesting late last night."

"What?". Hermione sounded doubtful.

"Mr Trent walking over the Green with Sadie. They were holding hands."

"Maybe they're just friends, taking a walk together" Hermione tried to keep her voice steady.

"I doubt it."

"Why not?"

"They were kissing and all sorts."

Eager as she was to make an official announcement that afternoon, Hermione knew that a little more research was necessary. Since Mr Trent was leaving in less than a week, she decided the speediest option was to befriend the hippy woman in the hope of extracting some concrete evidence. Having copied down the number from the card in Sarratt Stores window, she called the following day to book herself in for a bit of yoga. However Sadie told her that there were no yoga classes that week, but she was more than welcome to attend the "Getting in touch with your Inner Child" workshop on Friday.

Leaving her shoes by the front door as instructed, Hermione followed Sadie through to the sitting room, which was unlit apart from one candle. There was some strange music playing and Hermione could just about make out four or five figures lying prostrate on the floor. She found herself a spot as far away from anyone else as possible and lay down as Sadie told the group to spend the next fifteen minutes breathing deeply and emptying their minds. Hermione passed the time wondering how she could find an excuse to slip upstairs and check the bedroom for any tell tale signs of Mr Trent.

Sadie's voice interrupted her thoughts: "Now I want you to think back to a specific time in your childhood – a good time – a happy time. You may have been playing, dancing or singing, laughing, jumping, shouting. Whatever – Re-live the joy. Feel that emotion. Reach out for the inner child."

At this point the room seemed to awaken. People began shuffling around. A man on the far side of the room started singing to himself. Someone else was reciting a nursery rhyme. The woman next to Hermione was giggling like an imbecile, whilst kicking out with her legs, catching Hermione on the shin more than once.

Just as Hermione was wondering how much longer she'd be able to stick it out, Sadie cut in again: "I want you to think back to another time. A sad time. A hurtful time. A time, you have tried to forget. I'd like you to work through those feelings. Release those tears. Embrace the pain. Heal the wound."

The music, which up until that point, had been quite soothing, suddenly became a cacophony of horrendous, jarring sounds, triggering off a rather violent reaction. Bodies began to twist and writhe, grunting and moaning. The singing man started jumping up and down on the spot, shouting. The person on his left was clawing at the walls. Hermione's neighbour was now squealing like a stuck pig, but still lashing out with her legs. After a particularly nasty blow, Hermione decided she'd had enough. Seizing the opportunity when she sensed Sadie's back was turned, she raced for the front door, grabbing her shoes on the way. She didn't stop running until she was well past the Cricketers, so she didn't notice Mr Trent's Aston Martin pass by with a blonde girl in the passenger seat. And she was well out of earshot from the peals of laughter coming from Sadie's house.

Bathing her feet that evening, Hermione knew the likelihood of discovering the identity of Mr Trent's lover within next four days was at best, slim. Her only consolation was that Maureen Parker had been equally unsuccessful and at least there was the drinks party to look forward to.

By one o'clock on Saturday, the little gathering was in full swing. Much of the talk centred around the Trent affair and Annie Rawlins, who worked for News International said that if the story was true, a set of pictures showing the two together would be worth at least £75,000.

As soon as William turned up, Hermione grabbed his hand and marched him over to Sarah, who was discussing her latest play with Katie Staunton.

"William, you remember Sarah, don't you?"

"Yes, mother, I'm not simple. Hello Sarah. How's life in the world of luvvies."

"Fine. How's life in the world of cakes?"

"Great. Sorry, would you excuse me? I'm absolutely parched" and with that he walked off. Hermione waited for a full nine minutes, before trying again.

"William, if you've got a moment, I know Sarah would love to have a chat. She's thinking about a career in marketing, so any tips would be very welcome." Not strictly true but she'd sort that out later.

"Perhaps some other time. I've arranged to meet a friend for a drink this afternoon and I'm already late."

"Are you coming back?"

"Sorry, I've got plans for tonight. But I'll see you next weekend."

Hermione spent the rest of the drinks party bitterly resenting the £48.67 that she'd been forced into paying out for the fruitless gathering.

It was a call from Maureen Parker early on Sunday morning, which ruined the rest of Hermione's year.

"Have you seen the News of the World today?" she asked, "I think you'll find pages 2 and 3 quite interesting. By the way, I saw that your William holding hands with Donna Beggs in the Cock last night. What a sly old fox."

Hermione was still reeling as she opened The News of the World:

"Teenage temptress frolics with lusty star of Holland Park"
Dashing Hugh Trent has been caught cheating on his long term girlfriend Beth Hawley, with stable girl Debbie Lacey of Chipperfield. Busty Debbie (36 DD) has been spending nights of passion at Hugh's luxury rented house in the sleepy village of Sarratt in Hertfordshire..."

The piece was accompanied by a full double page spread of photos depicting Debbie romping with a naked Mr Trent in the swimming pool at Little Sarratt Hall.

* * *

Queenie stretched out in her British Airways seat and munched contentedly on her roasted peanuts. She was really looking forward to photographing the wildlife in Kenya and she fondly patted her new Nikon in the seat next to her. Strange that – when Maureen's son had first shown her the complicated looking camera with it's funny, long lens, she didn't think that she'd ever be able to work it, but after a bit of practice, she'd soon got the hang of it.

What I wanted was a name. Just one verifiable moniker. Someone who could be looked up in the records. A former High Sheriff, Justice of the Peace, businessman, bon-viveur and philanthropist – revealed as a spy for the KGB... But although Colonel Mikhail Lyubimov, thought by some to have been the prototype of le Carré's infamous Karla, retired from the world of espionage more than twenty years ago he was not about to spill the beans. "Even the ashes of the dead should be left undisturbed, in my opinion," he said, matter of factly.

This seemed a promising and entirely appropriate start to an interview in which Colonel Lyubimov had agreed to speak about his experiences as an agent. After all, what kind of a spy dishes the dirt? A malcontent, perhaps; not a professional. "Besides," he went on, "The history of espionage is a history of fiascos. One cannot speak about success in espionage." Quite. Secrets revealed denote failure. Success is the worm swallowed whole.

With his stage Russian accent, Colonel Lyubimov sounds splendidly sinister. He was a volunteer, not a recruit to the intelligence services, a fact which still surprises him somewhat. His father was himself a member of Stalin's infamous secret police, the Cheka. "I put myself forward in 1957 whilst I was still a student – just as your le Carré began working for M16 whilst he was a student at university in Bern.

"My first actual job as an agent was to seduce an American girl. I posed as a young professor from Kiev who was staying in the same hotel. The Metropole in Moscow: a preposterous idea! Nevertheless, it began very well. She was charmed with this young intellectual who wined her with champagne and dined her on caviar. We danced together before going upstairs to my room – which just happened to be on the same corridor as hers. Just as I was beginning to get down to my main task, the telephone rang. "Remove the chair!" came the order. I had forgotten about the camera and pulled up a chair over which I'd thrown my trousers.

"Well of course this precipitated a disaster for me as a man! She left very confused after such a promising start. The next day I went to the doctor and told him about my failure. I was convinced that I was impotent. (I was just 22 years old at the time.) He gave me an injection – no doubt water – and I walked out on air. I felt ready to take on all the women in the world. The second night, however, I made another blunder. In order to encourage this girl, I gave her what we call white beer – a mixture of champagne and brandy. As a result she became very ill. But now I was in love. Against all instructions I went into her room. (The KGB cannot install cameras everywhere. That's a myth.) This time, however it was the staff who were the problem. Although they were all agents themselves, not everybody knew what was going on. So when they saw this crazed Russian pursuing an unknown foreigner into her room they became very concerned. After a few minutes, a maid came in to "change the flowers". I fully expected to get into trouble. But instead all my boss said was "Never mind. You tried." I did not know who or what this young American was. That was never disclosed to agents. But that was my first job as a spy. And after that it was decided that I was "good for girls".

"I was then sent to Finland where I was given the task of seducing a girl who worked in the American embassy. But she was much too cautious and I ended up being sent back to Moscow and entering the cadre. I then went to intelligence school where I did nothing for two years. I already had a second language and a good education. Languages were the most important part of the new spy's training. Followed by political training. Only after this was complete did we get taught spy tricks.

"At the Russian equivalent of le Carré's "nursery" we learned firstly about things like how to avoid detection by making a proper plan first, how to "work" the bus and the metro and so on and how to discover a tail. For example, a successful rendezvous generally takes a minimum of two hours from arrival on site until the actual meeting. You have to have observation posts, counter-observation posts and so on.

"As far as recruiting foreign agents was concerned, it was a question firstly of making contacts. This is the most important aspect. Without contacts you can do nothing so this entails learning how to talk to people, how and where to socialize with potential recruits and so on. Next there is cultivation of these contacts. This is usually very difficult. I used to meet a lot of journalists but probably only one in ten would agree to meet further. And only one in twenty or thirty would agree to keep the meeting secret. "Listen," I would say, "don't phone the embassy. Meet me in Kew Gardens."

"Then came recruiting, of which there are two kinds. There is overt recruitment of course. Then there is recruitment where the person does not realize they are being recruited. For example, I might suggest to someone, perhaps an academic, "Would you be interested to write an article?" "What sort of an article?" "Well we have a journal which is more or less confidential..." He or she is offered a fee. They get interested. But what they don't realize is that their articles are considered to be reports. And at the same time they are gradually drawn in.

"Sometimes the recruiting is open. For example I remember meeting a British trade unionist in Moscow. He was so far to the left it should actually have been him who was recruiting me! When I mentioned that I was connected with the KGB and asked him about political co-operation he was almost overwhelmed. "At last!" he exclaimed.

"Our training also covered working with agents. Some of these are of course inherited. Here for example I think of one Englishman I worked with. He had been very important to us during the war – not a member of the Cambridge group – but middle-class, someone who had fought with the International Brigade during the Spanish civil war. He had subsequently come over to us in disgust at Chamberlain's Munich agreement. A very nice man and a true ideologue. He worked in the press and supplied us with such important information from the various foreign embassies he had dealings with that he was awarded the Order of Lenin – then the highest award in Russia. But I cannot say more. It might cause trouble for his relatives if his identity were known."

"How did we know whom to trust? How could he know which were genuine recruits and which were merely stooges?"

"Of course, knowing where someone's true loyalty lies is the hardest task. But it is not confined to one's agents: it extends to everyone we have dealings with. Nevertheless, we had methods designed to check up on people to which we subjected all our agents once or twice a year. So for example we might say to agent J "My dear David would you be so kind as to take this bag with you to such and such a meeting? When you get there, just push this button." What the agent does not realise is that the case is fitted with another device. When he goes home and picks up the phone and says "Guess what. That bloody Russian has given me a bag that I'm supposed to take into the meeting" it records the conversation.

"In connection with this, I remember one occasion when we suspected an agent of being a stooge. So we arranged for him to pick up a canister from a dead letter box and hand it back to us. It was chemically treated so that we could tell whether it had been opened or not. Seven times we repeated this. It wasn't until the eighth time that the seal came back broken. That was the end of the agent of course. But it says something for the patience of M15. They were almost supernaturally patient. They were also extremely good at the way they handled people they knew to be working for us. Even today I have many doubts about which of my agents were known to M15 and which were not."

"Similarly, the British always dealt very nicely with those they discovered working for us. Philby, Burgess and Maclean could all have been arrested. But they were merely told that the game was up and that was that."

"At the time that I was in London, our main enemy was the US. Accordingly what we most wanted was information concerning relations between Britain and America – strains in NATO which could be exploited, things like that. We also wanted to know about the attitude of the British government towards Russia. We wanted information about British agents working in Russia. And we wanted information about technical and military developments. To this latter end, for example, we ran many agents at Porton Down, the research centre for Nuclear, Biological and Chemical warfare."

"So far as recruitment is concerned, if you look at your own agents in Russia, you will see that yes, some came to you for money or through blackmail. But mainly they were dissidents, anti-Soviets. So clearly ideology is the most significant factor. At the same time, it is a mistake to think there is such a thing as "pure" ideology. It is almost invariably fortified by money or the granting of privileges. Take an MP who is put up for a month in a hotel in the Caucasus. It is a question of making people feel obliged. Exploiting human nature is your job."

"But espionage is more of a style of life than merely a job – people do it best when it is their style of life. To illustrate what I mean, take the example of one friend of mine. He is a spy wherever he goes and under whatever circumstance. We are looking for somewhere to eat in Moscow and we come to an Azerbaijani restaurant. There is a queue waiting to get in. He goes up to the doorman and asks whether Mr Ali has telephoned? Which Mr Ali? You mean there is another Mr Ali, he says significantly. We are immediately shown to a table. As we are leaving he goes up to the pretty girl he has been looking at and hands her his card. "I need you for my next film, he says. I'm a director of Moscfilm. Call me." Outside we see a car waiting. He goes up to the driver and tells him "The Boss" says to take us home." That man is a spy through and through. A real adventurer, living on his wits all the time."

"But nowadays I have the sense that there's a lot of routine bureaucracy. If you want to recruit somebody you have to ask plenty of seniors. Then there are papers to be written, approved, discussed. It's not the same. But when I was a young agent in England I was completely free to go wherever I wanted. Of course I was watched. That only changed when I became the head man in London. Thereafter I was no longer free. My life became taken up with administration, co-ordination and so forth. I should have stopped at that point. But I stayed another ten years, until I became pensionable at the age of 46. And by that time my conversion was complete. I was a bourgeois."

Mikhail Lyubimov, friend of Philby, Blake and Cairncross stubbed out his Cuban cheroot insouciantly. I felt a little uneasy. This was the only part of his story that didn't quite ring true. We were lunching at one of the Roux brothers' famous restaurants. Judging by his charm and the ease with which he conducted himself amidst such luxurious surroundings, it was hard to believe he hadn't been a bourgeois all along.

Alexander Norman has written extensively for The Spectator, The Financial Times *and* The Daily Mail. *He co-wrote both the Dalai Lama's autobiography* Freedom in Exile *and the Dalai Lama's current bestselling* 'Ancient Wisdom, Modern World'.

*The Rev. Edward Ryley M.A. Rector 1859-1912 wrote this short history
97 years ago and it was read by him at the Church of the Holy Cross
to members of the St. Albans & Herts Architectural and Archeological
Society on 7th September 1902. It is included in this book slightly
abridged as we believe it is of no less interest today.*

The ancient church is dedicated to the Holy Cross and its structure
well fulfils its name as, till the restoration in 1865, it was in the
form of a true Greek Cross. The name of the village was then
spelt Sarrett or Syret, from a Swedish family of three brothers
who came over in the 8th century, as tradition had it. Chauncy says "Offa,
King of the Mercians, granted this Vill of Syret now called Sarratt to the
Monastery of St. Albans, anno 796 33 Regni sui, so called from Syret, a
Saxon, who I suppose was an ancient possessor of it. Some explain the
name as meaning the road by the water as, in treading the parish
boundaries a man called the water-dog used to wade through the middle
of the stream, the river Chess, which separates Sarratt from the county
of Bucks. Others derive the word from the Saxon Shiregate, or Shire Gate
meaning the parish approach to the county of Bucks. The exact date of
this church, which is considered to be the most interesting in the Rural
Deanery of Watford, is uncertain. As soon as I was instituted here in 1859,
I tried to find out the approximate date and for that purpose went to the
reading room of the British Museum. I consulted and took extracts from
the Histories of Clutterbuck, Salmon, Chauncy and from other histories,
e.g. from a printed portion of Cox's Magna Britannica, date 1725.

However, this church has a reputation of being 800 years old[*], according
to archeologists, who style it transition Norman: but you see there is
nothing decidedly Norman about it, though that late prince of modern
architects, Sir Gilbert Scott, who restored it during my incumbency in
1865-6, traced by the abaci mouldings in the chancel the remains of
Norman architecture; and the west window in the tower, he distinctly
told me, was of older date than Westminster Abbey. The walls are of flint

---

[*]Editors note: Now believed to have been built in 1190 AD, and thus just over 700 years old in 1902.

throughout and three feet thick with the exception of the mouldings of arches and windows which are of Totternhoe stone.

The church in 1859 was in a most dilapidated and deplorable state but Sir Gilbert Scott, who worshipped in this church as a boy and who, in consequence, naturally took a great interest in it, kept to the original details as much as possible, keeping to the old massive structure and introducing nothing tawdry or florid. The old pulpit is unique both as to structure and size and that it is older than the well-known one at St. Michael's, St. Albans. It is Jacobean and the carving on the body on it is designated as the linen pattern; this, together with the sounding-board is worth examination. It is, I believe, a specimen of one of the oldest pulpits in England.

In 1864 I determined to have a thorough restoration as the roof and ceiling, of barrel shape, which I had had temporarily repaired to keep out the rain and daylight, were in bad condition. The walls were green and dangerous and the floors all in holes and uneven and an extended or opened-out cheese box was used to keep out the draughts through the front door. All the oak beams and rafters were brought to light and repaired and new ones inserted where necessary both in the body of the church and chancel. The entrance to the north transept which was blocked partly by a large board of the parish charities and by lath and plaster between the abaci of a former arch was opened; several new arches were erected and the supporting pillars were built on a gravel foundation nine feet deep.

The north side was covered with yellow frescoes of fruits and flowers, pomegranates and pineapples but too friable for repair. On the chancel arch in the body of the church an old bricklayer told me he had whitewashed numbers of Kings and Queens, as he called them; these I have not attempted to uncover, the wall is too decayed; but on the east wall of the south transept I did attempt some work with my pen-knife and brought to view what may be called the life of our Lord from His birth to his ascension.

During the restoration, when any foundations were dug, I had the gravel carefully sifted and there were found one little bit of a painted window and two small coins of Charles I's time. This leads me to

Above: The Holy Cross Church showing the tower with the saddle-back roof.
Below left: The lecturn and part of the Jacobean pulpit with the linenfold carving.
Below right: A section of pudding stone under the tower and the Clutterbuck tomb.

the fact that this church was built on the site of a Roman cemetery. The Romans often loved a spot with a fair view on the brow of a hill and I have constantly unearthed pieces of cinerary urns or vases while in one deep grave I found a true Roman key and a small Roman brooch. Under the new porch were found portions of a stone coffin of Purbeck marble and a coffin lid of free stone is placed on the ground near the vestry window which has a floriated cross on it and is considered as belonging to the 13th century. I may mention that there are three bells: the oldest 1606, with the inscription "Knight made me in 1606", the second "Chandlers made me in 1719", and the third by Mears and Stainbank, 1865; this last took the place of an old one that, unfortunately, before my incumbency, was taken down and sold for old brass at Chenies where there was a foundry.

And now let me allude to the principal peculiarity of Holy Cross Church – I mean the almost unique tower with its so-called saddle-back roof; there are, I believe, only three other churches which have the roof of the tower facing north and south. The foundation stone of the tower is a fine specimen of conglomerate so-called Hertfordshire pudding stone or breeding-stone and there are others like it hard by. Though the tower is a brick one at the top, it is considered to be the original.

In 1859 there were no foundations, the church rested on the ground; so at the restoration the whole church was under-pinned and water pipes placed three feet under as drainage; spouts or gutters also were added. The entire restoration cost £1400 and the architect expressed himself afterwards as well satisfied with the substantial work.

Originally the old church must have presented internally a stately appearance with its beautifully frescoed walls and well-tiled flooring. You will see I have preserved a few of the best of the ancient tiles and placed twelve of these relics of departed glory in the chancel in front of the communion table. The old register dates from 1560 or the second year of Queen Elizabeth's reign.

Cow Parsley After Rain By Agnes Bantock

63

In the preparation of this book we are indebted above all to John le Carré who by siting "The Nursery" at Sarratt thereby sparked off the whole idea.

Likewise our thanks to the other writers and artists and the multitude of helpers who have contributed in so many ways. We list below everybody we can think of but there are countless others who have in turn assisted those named.

There will also be many more although they do not really know it yet!

As with so many towns and villages, in Sarratt, when there is a job to be done of benefit to the community there is a remarkable unsung army who just pitch in and help.

In this case selling, packing, posting and accounting for the stock and sales in the coming months. Our thanks to all of you.

Agnes Bantock	Dick Edmonds	Mikhail Lyubimov
Philip Beausire	Hattie Edmonds	Alexander Norman
The Biggerstaff family	Michael Edmund	William Petre
Gillian Burrows	Roy Eteen	Michael Rogers
John le Carré	Natasha Franklin	Doris Rollinson
Michael Clark	Philip Gooding	Kate Saunders
David Clough	John Guy	Muir Stratford
Jan Clutterbuck	Gill Harmon	Pam Turner
Shirley Cordery	Peter Hart	Robert Walker
Val Cumming	Michael Hewlett	Bruce Weindruch
Ian Dorrett	Bruce Hunter	Grelle White
Roger Dudley	Stephen Lawrence	Kurt Willinger

Finally, the book is dedicated to all who live in Sarratt now and moreover to future generations whom we hope will treasure the countryside and the traditions of this English village.

Photograph on P.10 © Chris Chapman.
The book jacket is printed on Sensation Natural White 170 gsm supplied by The Creative Link.

Dennis Jenks *Editor*
Michael O'Donnell *Designer*   October 1999